Desert Song

by Tony Johnston
Illustrations by Ed Young

Sierra Club Books for Children
San Francisco

The Sierra Club, founded in 1892 by John Muir, has devoted itself to the study and protection of the earth's scenic and ecological resources — mountains, wetlands, woodlands, wild shores and rivers, deserts and plains. The publishing program of the Sierra Club offers books to the public as a nonprofit educational service in the hope that they may enlarge the public's understanding of the Club's basic concerns. The point of view expressed in each book, however, does not necessarily represent that of the Club. The Sierra Club has some sixty chapters in the United States and Canada. For information about how you may participate in its programs to preserve wilderness and the quality of life, please address inquiries to Sierra Club, 85 Second Street, San Francisco, CA 94105, or visit our website at www.sierraclub.org.

First Edition

Published by Sierra Club Books for Children
85 Second Street, San Francisco, California 94105
www.sierraclub.org/books

Published in conjunction with Gibbs Smith, Publisher
P.O. Box 667, Layton Utah 84041
www.gibbs-smith.com

Library of Congress Cataloging-in-Publicaton Data

Johnston, Tony.
    Desert song / by Tony Johnston; illustrations by Ed Young.
— 1st ed.
        p. cm.
        Summary: As the heat of the desert day fades into night,
various nocturnal animals, including bats, coyotes, and
snakes, venture out to find food.
        ISBN 0-87156-491-2 (alk paper)
        1. Desert animals Juvenile fiction. [1. Desert animals
Fiction. 2. Bats Fiction.] I. Young, Ed, ill. II. Title.
PZ10.3.J715De 2000
[E] — dc21   99-36886

Art direction by Nanette Stevenson
Title lettering by David Gatti

Printed in Hong Kong

10 9 8 7 6 5 4 3 2 1

For Ann Bustard,
who shared Austin's bats with me
— T.J.

For French Conway,
a friend and a naturalist
— E.Y.

Day is done.
Twilight comes.
The sun goes down
and streaks the clouds
with flame.

The melting heat
is gone.
It leaves
its last warm breath
wavering
over the land.

A quail calls
from a shaded hiding place.

Day is done.
Twilight comes.

Suddenly
with a rush of wings
bats spill from a cave
in a hill.

They have been sleeping
all day long.
Now they pour
into the night
like dry leaves
blowing,
like shadows
on the wing.

They soar.
They race
across the silent sweep of sand,
their small mouse faces
thrust into the wind.

Everywhere
deepening night
is full of insects flying
or creeping
along the ground —
moths and ants,
weevils,
beetles —
seeking the saguaro's
sweet fruit.

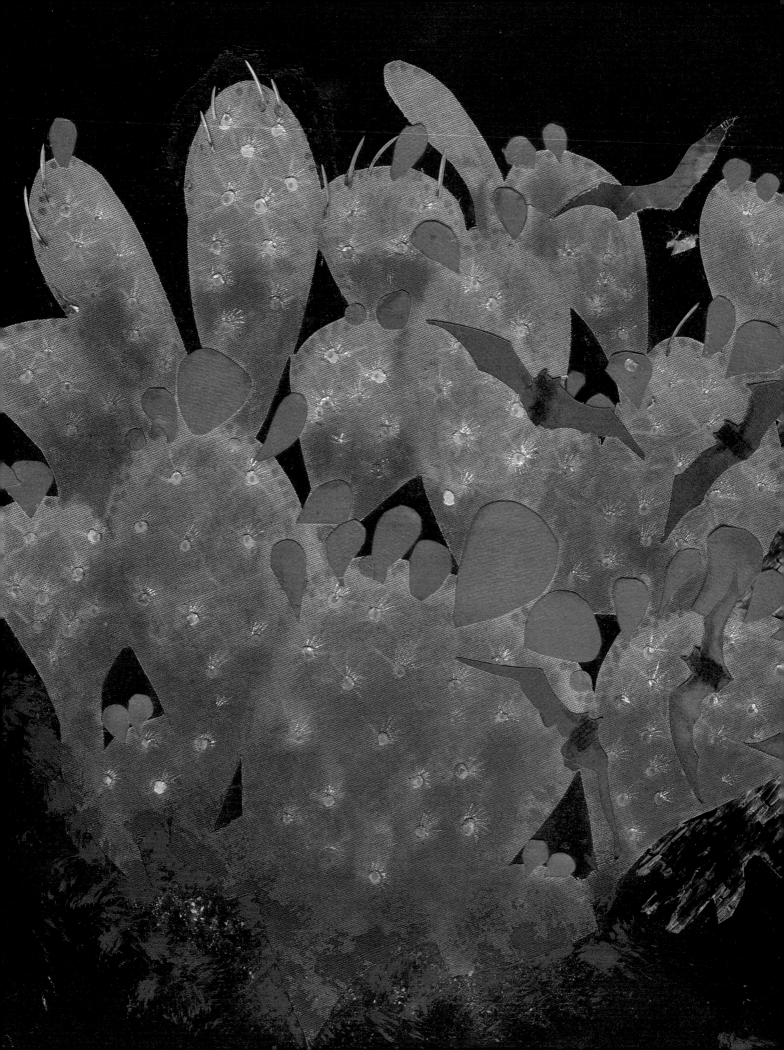

Whirrrrrrrr.

Everywhere
the air is full of bats
squeaking,
seeking
insects to eat.

They dip their wings
like swallows
swooping low.

And they hunt.

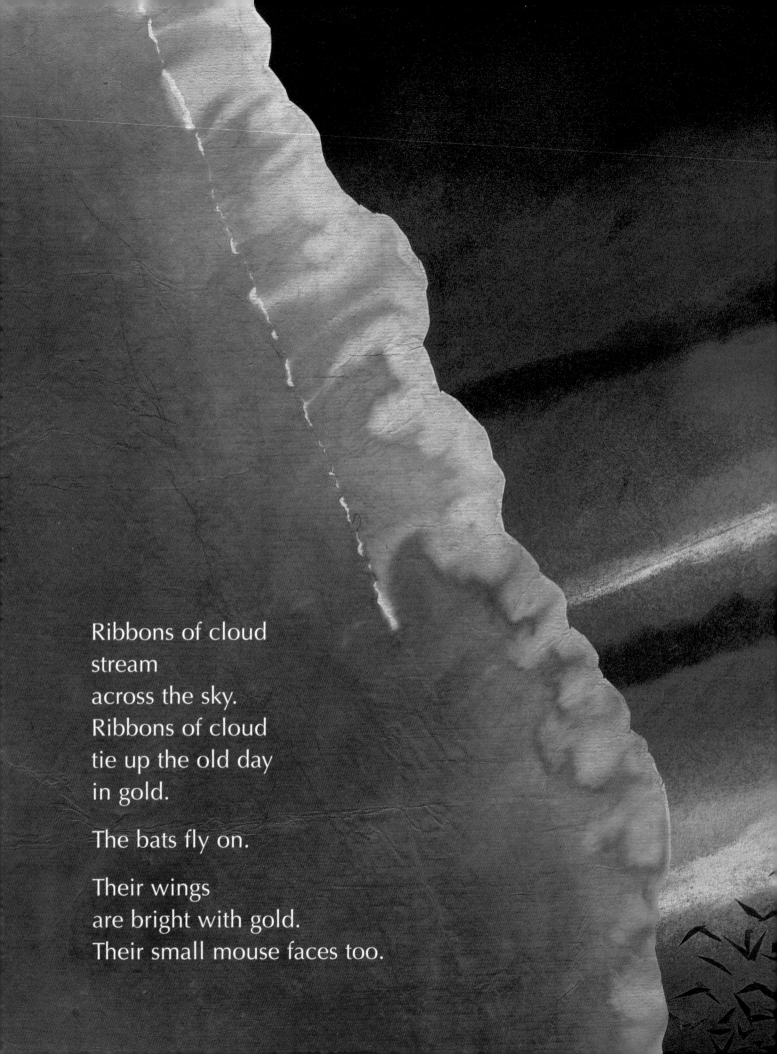

Ribbons of cloud
stream
across the sky.
Ribbons of cloud
tie up the old day
in gold.

The bats fly on.

Their wings
are bright with gold.
Their small mouse faces too.

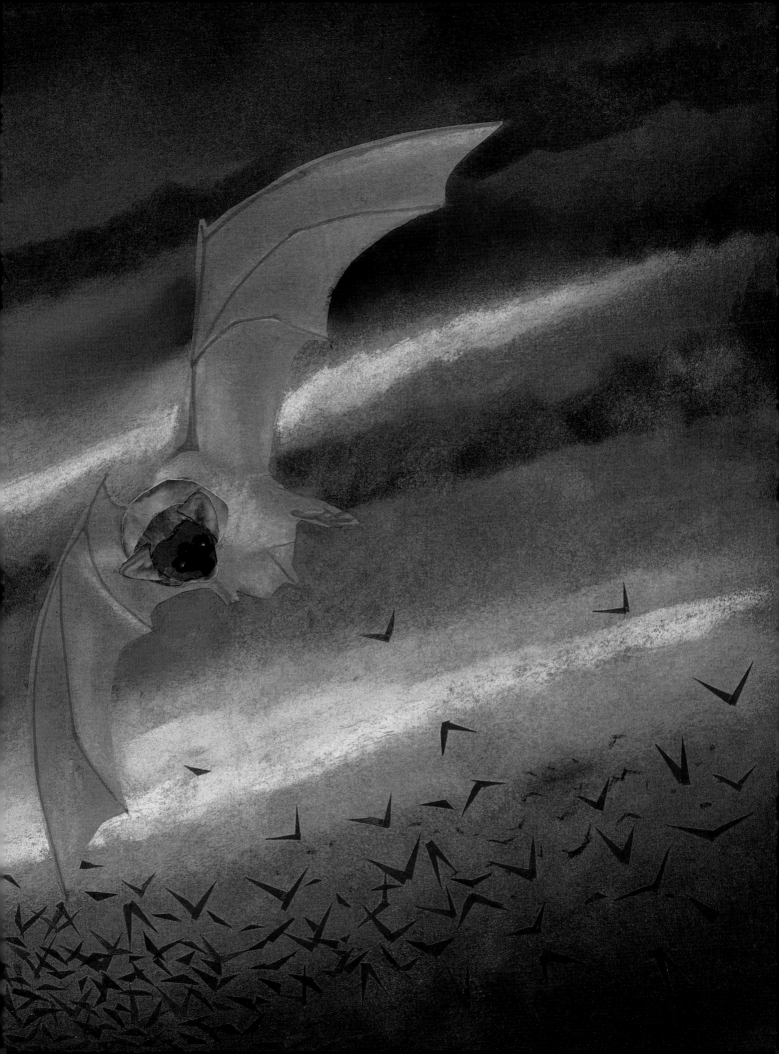

The wind whispers.
Wings whisper
as insects fly through the night,
and the bats fly
hunting them

under countless stars,
along wrinkled hills,
over the desert
sharp with spikes
and spines
and prongs.

The desert fills
with songs.

From a scrawny plant
an owl hoots
one kind of song
as it hunts.

A coyote hunts too.
He prowls
among the spines and prongs.
Then he stops to sing
to the moon.

Song of wonder.
Song of hunger.
Song of being alone.

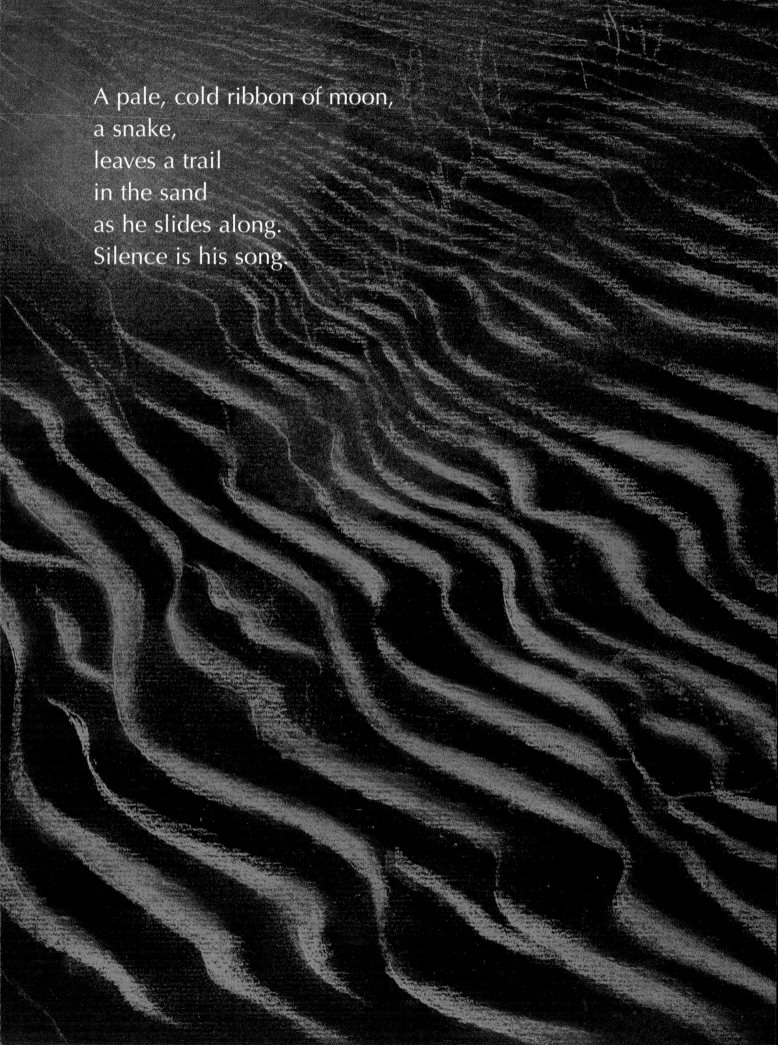

A pale, cold ribbon of moon,
a snake,
leaves a trail
in the sand
as he slides along.
Silence is his song.

Now one star
in the thinning dark
still glows.

Now morning blooms.

Now many flowers open.
Now many flowers close.

Night things
slip into the cool
of desert hiding places.
They slip into pools of shade,
coyote
and owl
and snake.

As nighttime insects disappear,
the bats fly home
across the silent sweep of sand.

Home to the darkness,
home to their hungry young,
home to a cave
in a hill.

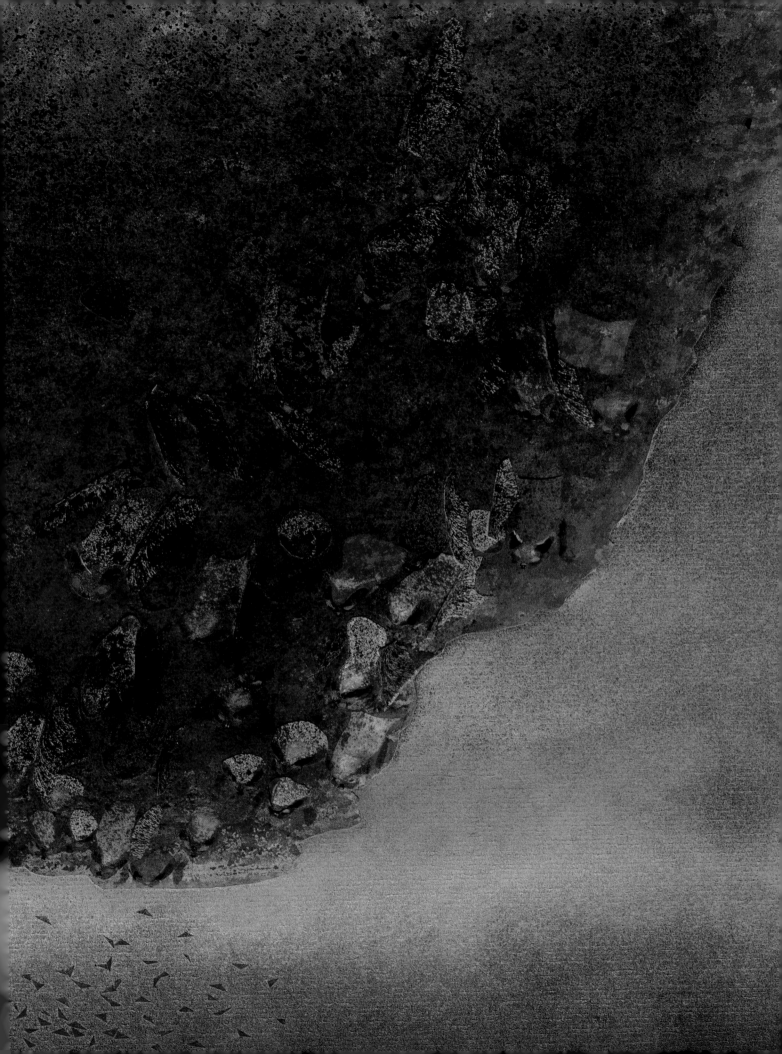

They sleep then,
clustered
close and still,
until day is done
and the sun goes down
and twilight comes again.